THE SOUL OF THE INDIAN

An Interpretation

THE VISION

THE SOUL OF THE INDIAN

An Interpretation

BY

CHARLES ALEXANDER EASTMAN

(OHIYESA)

AUTHOR OF "INDIAN BOYHOOD," ETC

ISBN: 978-93-5128-507-6(HB)

First Published in 1911
Indian Reprint in 2017

Published by

Kalpaz Publications
C-30, Satyawati Nagar,
Delhi – 110052
E-mail: kalpaz@hotmail.com
Website: kalpazpublications.com
Ph.: +91-9212142040

Cataloging in Publication Data—DK
Courtesy: D.K. Agencies (P) Ltd. <docinfo@dkagencies.com>

Eastman, Charles A., 1858-1939, **author.**
The soul of the Indian : an interpretation/by Charles Alexander Eastman (Ohiyesa).
pages cm
"First published in 1911"—Title page verso.
ISBN 9789351285076

1. Indians of North America—Religion. I. Title.

E98.R3E27 2017 DDC 299.7 23

TO MY WIFE

ELAINE GOODALE EASTMAN

IN GRATEFUL RECOGNITION OF HER

EVER-INSPIRING COMPANIONSHIP

IN THOUGHT AND WORK

AND IN LOVE OF HER MOST

INDIAN-LIKE VIRTUES

I DEDICATE THIS BOOK

I speak for each no-tongued tree
That, spring by spring, doth nobler be,
And dumbly and most wistfully
His mighty prayerful arms outspreads,
And his big blessing downward sheds.

SIDNEY LANIER.

But there's a dome of nobler span,
        A temple given
Thy faith, that bigots dare not ban—
        Its space is heaven!
It's roof star-pictured Nature's ceiling,
Where, trancing the rapt spirit's feeling,
And God Himself to man revealing,
        Th' harmonious spheres
Make music, though unheard their pealing
        By mortal ears!

THOMAS CAMPBELL.

God! sing ye meadow streams with gladsome voice!
Ye pine-groves, with your soft and soul-like sounds!
Ye eagles, playmates of the mountain storm!
Ye lightnings, the dread arrows of the clouds!
Ye signs and wonders of the elements,
Utter forth God, and fill the hills with praise!...
Earth, with her thousand voices, praises GOD!

COLERIDGE.

FOREWORD

"We also have a religion which was given to our forefathers, and has been handed down to us their children. It teaches us to be thankful, to be united, and to love one another! We never quarrel about religion."

Thus spoke the great Seneca orator, Red Jacket, in his superb reply to Missionary Cram more than a century ago, and I have often heard the same thought expressed by my countrymen.

I have attempted to paint the religious life of the typical American Indian as it was before he knew the white man. I have long wished to do this, because I cannot find that it has ever been seriously, adequately, and sincerely done. The religion of the Indian is the last thing about him that the man of another race will ever understand.

First, the Indian does not speak of these deep matters so long as he believes in them, and when he has ceased to believe he speaks inaccurately and slightingly.

Second, even if he can be induced to speak, the racial and religious prejudice of the other stands in the way of his sympathetic comprehension.

Third, practically all existing studies on this subject have been made during the transition period, when the original beliefs and philosophy of the native American were already undergoing rapid disintegration.

There are to be found here and there superficial accounts of strange customs and ceremonies, of which the symbolism or inner meaning was largely hidden from the observer; and there has been a great deal of material collected in recent years which is without value because it is modern and hybrid, inextricably mixed with Biblical legend and Caucasian philosophy. Some of it has even been invented for commercial purposes. Give a reservation Indian a present, and he will possibly provide you with sacred songs, a mythology, and folk-lore to order!

My little book does not pretend to be a scientific treatise. It is as true as I can make it to my childhood teaching and ancestral ideals, but from the human, not the ethnological standpoint. I have not cared to pile up more dry bones, but to clothe them with flesh and blood. So much as has been written by strangers of our ancient faith and worship treats it chiefly as matter of curiosity. I should like to emphasize its universal quality, its personal appeal!

FOREWORD

The first missionaries, good men imbued with the narrow-ness of their age, branded us as pagans and devil-worshipers, and demanded of us that we abjure our false gods before bowing the knee at their sacred altar. They even told us that we were eternally lost, unless we adopted a tangible symbol and professed a particular form of their hydra-headed faith.

We of the twentieth century know better! We know that all religious aspiration, all sincere worship, can have but one source and one goal. We know that the God of the lettered and the unlettered, of the Greek and the barbarian, is after all the same God; and, like Peter, we perceive that He is no respecter of persons, but that in every nation he that feareth Him and worketh righteousness is acceptable to Him.

Charles A. Eastman (Ohiyesa)

CONTENTS

I

THE GREAT MYSTERY

Solitary Worship. The Savage Philosopher. The Dual Mind. Spiritual Gifts *versus* Material Progress. The Paradox of "Christian Civilization."

The original attitude of the American Indian toward the Eternal, the "Great Mystery" that surrounds and embraces us, was as simple as it was exalted. To him it was the supreme conception, bringing with it the fullest measure of joy and satisfaction possible in this life.

The worship of the "Great Mystery" was silent, solitary, free from all self-seeking. It was silent, because all speech is of necessity feeble and imperfect; therefore the souls of my ancestors ascended to God in wordless adoration. It was solitary, because they believed that He is nearer to us in solitude, and there were no priests authorized to come between a man and his Maker. None might exhort or confess or in any way meddle with the religious experience of another. Among us all men were created sons of God and stood erect, as conscious of their divinity. Our faith might not be formulated in creeds, nor forced upon any who were unwilling to receive it; hence there was no preaching, proselyting, nor persecution, neither were there any scoffers or atheists.

There were no temples or shrines among us save those of nature. Being a natural man, the Indian was intensely poetical. He would deem it sacrilege to build a house for Him who may be met face to face in the mysterious, shadowy aisles of the primeval forest, or on the sunlit bosom of virgin prairies, upon dizzy spires and pinnacles of naked rock, and yonder in the jeweled vault of the night sky! He who enrobes Himself in filmy veils of cloud, there on the rim of the visible world where our Great-Grandfather Sun kindles his evening camp-fire, He who rides upon the rigorous wind of the north, or breathes forth His spirit upon aromatic southern airs, whose war-canoe is launched upon majestic rivers and inland seas—He needs no lesser cathedral!

That solitary communion with the Unseen which was the highest expression of our religious life is partly described in the word *bambeday,* literally "mysterious feeling," which has been variously translated "fasting" and "dreaming." It may better be interpreted as "consciousness of the divine."

The first *bambeday*, or religious retreat, marked an epoch in the life of the youth, which may be compared to that of confirmation or conversion in Christian experience. Having first prepared himself by means of the purifying vapor-bath, and cast off as far as possible all human or fleshly influences, the young man sought out the noblest height, the most commanding summit in all the surrounding region. Knowing that God sets no value upon material things, he took with him no offerings or sacrifices other than symbolic objects, such as paints and tobacco. Wishing to appear before Him in all humility, he wore no clothing save his moccasins and breech-clout. At the solemn hour of sunrise or sunset he took up his position, overlooking the glories of earth and facing the "Great Mystery," and there he remained, naked, erect, silent, and motionless, exposed to the elements and forces of His arming, for a night and a day to two days and nights, but rarely longer. Sometimes he would chant a hymn without words, or offer the ceremonial "filled pipe." In this holy trance or ecstasy the Indian mystic found his highest happiness and the motive power of his existence.

When he returned to the camp, he must remain at a distance until he had again entered the vapor-bath and prepared himself for intercourse with his fellows. Of the vision or sign vouchsafed to him he did not speak, unless it had included some commission which must be publicly fulfilled. Sometimes an old man, standing upon the brink of eternity, might reveal to a chosen few the oracle of his long-past youth.

The native American has been generally despised by his white conquerors for his poverty and simplicity. They forget, perhaps, that his religion forbade the accumulation of wealth and the enjoyment of luxury. To him, as to other single-minded men in every age and race, from Diogenes to the brothers of Saint Francis, from the Montanists to the Shakers, the love of possessions has appeared a snare, and the burdens of a complex society a source of needless peril and temptation. Furthermore, it was the rule of his life to share the fruits of his skill and success with his less fortunate brothers. Thus he kept his spirit free from the clog of pride, cupidity, or envy, and carried out, as he believed, the divine decree—a matter profoundly important to him.

It was not, then, wholly from ignorance or improvidence that he failed to establish permanent towns and to develop a material civilization. To the untutored sage, the concentration of population was the prolific mother of all evils, moral no less than physical. He argued that food is good, while surfeit kills; that love is good, but lust destroys; and not less dreaded than the pestilence following upon crowded and unsanitary dwellings was the loss of spiritual power inseparable from too close contact with one's fellow-men. All who have lived much out of doors know that there is a magnetic and nervous force that accumulates in solitude and that is quickly dissipated by life in a crowd; and even his enemies have recognized the fact that for a certain innate power and self-poise, wholly independent of circumstances, the American Indian is unsurpassed among men.

The red man divided mind into two parts,—the spiritual mind and the physical mind. The first is pure spirit, concerned only with the essence of things, and it was this he sought to strengthen by spiritual prayer, during which the body is subdued by fasting and hardship. In this type of prayer there was no beseeching of favor or help. All matters of personal or selfish concern, as success in hunting or warfare, relief from sickness, or the sparing of a beloved life, were definitely relegated to the plane of the lower or material mind, and all ceremonies, charms, or incantations designed to secure a benefit or to avert a danger, were recognized as emanating from the physical self.

The rites of this physical worship, again, were wholly symbolic, and the Indian no more worshiped the Sun than the Christian adores the Cross. The Sun and the Earth, by an obvious parable, holding scarcely more of poetic metaphor than of scientific truth, were in his view the parents of all organic life. From the Sun, as the universal father, proceeds the quickening principle in nature, and in the patient and fruitful womb of our mother, the Earth, are hidden embryos of plants and men. Therefore our reverence and love for them was really an imaginative extension of our love for our immediate parents, and with this sentiment of filial piety was joined a willingness to appeal to them, as to a father, for such good gifts as we may desire. This is the material or physical prayer.

The elements and majestic forces in nature, Lightning, Wind, Water, Fire, and Frost, were regarded with awe as spiritual powers, but always secondary and intermediate in character. We believed that the spirit pervades all creation and that every creature possesses a soul in some degree, though not necessarily a soul conscious of itself. The tree, the waterfall, the grizzly bear, each is an embodied Force, and as such an object of reverence.

The Indian loved to come into sympathy and spiritual communion with his brothers of the animal kingdom, whose inarticulate souls had for him something of the sinless purity that we attribute to the innocent and irresponsible child. He had faith in their instincts, as in a mysterious wisdom given from above; and while he humbly accepted the supposedly voluntary sacrifice of their bodies to preserve his own, he paid homage to their spirits in prescribed prayers and offerings.

In every religion there is an element of the supernatural, varying with the influence of pure reason over its devotees. The Indian was a logical and clear thinker upon matters within the scope of his understanding, but he had not yet charted the vast field of nature or expressed her wonders in terms of science. With his limited knowledge of cause and effect, he saw miracles on every hand,—the miracle of life in seed and egg, the miracle of death in lightning flash and in the swelling deep! Nothing of the marvelous could astonish him; as that a beast should speak, or the sun stand still. The virgin birth would appear scarcely more miraculous than is the birth of every child that comes into the world, or the miracle of the loaves and fishes excite more wonder than the harvest that springs from a single ear of corn.

Who may condemn his superstition? Surely not the devout Catholic, or even Protestant missionary, who teaches Bible miracles as literal fact! The logical man must either deny all miracles or none, and our American Indian myths and hero stories are perhaps, in themselves, quite as credible as those of the Hebrews of old. If we are of the modern type of mind, that sees in natural law a majesty and grandeur far more impressive than any solitary infraction of it could possibly be, let us not forget that, after all, science has not explained everything. We have still to face the ultimate miracle,—the origin and principle of life! Here is the supreme mystery that is the essence of worship, without which there can be no religion, and in the presence of this mystery our attitude cannot be very unlike that of the natural philosopher, who beholds with awe the Divine in all creation.

It is simple truth that the Indian did not, so long as his native philosophy held sway over his mind, either envy or desire to imitate the splendid achievements of the white man. In his own thought he rose superior to them! He scorned them, even as a lofty spirit absorbed in its stern task rejects the soft beds, the luxurious food, the pleasure-worshiping dalliance of a rich neighbor. It was clear to him that virtue and happiness are independent of these things, if not incompatible with them.

There was undoubtedly much in primitive Christianity to appeal to this man, and Jesus' hard sayings to the rich and about the rich would have been entirely comprehensible to him. Yet the religion that is preached in our churches and practiced by our congregations, with its element of display and self-aggrandizement, its active proselytism, and its open contempt of all religions but its own, was for a long time extremely repellent. To his simple mind, the professionalism of the pulpit, the paid exhorter, the moneyed church, was an unspiritual and unedifying thing, and it was not until his spirit was broken and his moral and physical constitution undermined by trade, conquest, and strong drink, that Christian missionaries obtained any real hold upon him. Strange as it may seem, it is true that the proud pagan in his secret soul despised the good men who came to convert and to enlighten him!

Nor were its publicity and its Phariseeism the only elements in the alien religion that offended the red man. To him, it appeared shocking and almost incredible that there were among this people who claimed superiority many irreligious, who did not even pretend to profess the national faith. Not only did they not profess it, but they stooped so low as to insult their God with profane and sacrilegious speech! In our own tongue His name was not spoken aloud, even with utmost reverence, much less lightly or irreverently.

More than this, even in those white men who professed religion we found much inconsistency of conduct. They spoke much of spiritual things, while seeking only the material. They bought and sold everything: time, labor, personal independence, the love of woman, and even the ministrations of their holy faith! The lust for money, power, and conquest so characteristic of the Anglo-Saxon race did not escape moral condemnation at the hands of his untutored judge, nor did he fail to contrast this conspicuous trait of the dominant race with the spirit of the meek and lowly Jesus.

He might in time come to recognize that the drunkards and licentious among white men, with whom he too frequently came in contact, were condemned by the white man's religion as well, and must not be held to discredit it. But it was not so easy to overlook or to excuse national bad faith. When distinguished emissaries from the Father at Washington, some of them ministers of the gospel and even bishops, came to the Indian nations, and pledged to them in solemn treaty the national honor, with prayer and mention of their God; and when such treaties, so made, were promptly and shamelessly broken, is it strange that the action should arouse not only anger, but contempt? The historians of the white race admit that the Indian was never the first to repudiate his oath.

It is my personal belief, after thirty-five years' experience of it, that there is no such thing as "Christian civilization." I believe that Christianity and modern civilization are opposed and irreconcilable, and that the spirit of Christianity and of our ancient religion is essentially the same.

II

THE FAMILY ALTAR

Pre-natal Influence. Early Religious Teaching. The Function of the Aged. Woman, Marriage and the Family. Loyalty, Hospitality, Friendship.

The American Indian was an individualist in religion as in war. He had neither a national army nor an organized church. There was no priest to assume responsibility for another's soul. That is, we believed, the supreme duty of the parent, who only was permitted to claim in some degree the priestly office and function, since it is his creative and protecting power which alone approaches the solemn function of Deity.

The Indian was a religious man from his mother's womb. From the moment of her recognition of the fact of conception to the end of the second year of life, which was the ordinary duration of lactation, it was supposed by us that the mother's spiritual influence counted for most. Her attitude and secret meditations must be such as to instill into the receptive soul of the unborn child the love of the "Great Mystery" and a sense of brotherhood with all creation. Silence and isolation are the rule of life for the expectant mother. She wanders prayerful in the stillness of great woods, or on the bosom of the untrodden prairie, and to her poetic mind the immanent birth of her child prefigures the advent of a master-man—a hero, or the mother of heroes—a thought conceived in the virgin breast of primeval nature, and dreamed out in a hush that is only broken by the sighing of the pine tree or the thrilling orchestra of a distant waterfall.

And when the day of days in her life dawns—the day in which there is to be a new life, the miracle of whose making has been intrusted to her, she seeks no human aid. She has been trained and prepared in body and mind for this her holiest duty, ever since she can remember. The ordeal is best met alone, where no curious or pitying eyes embarrass her; where all nature says to her spirit: "'Tis love! 'tis love! the fulfilling of life!" When a sacred voice comes to her out of the silence, and a pair of eyes open upon her in the wilderness, she knows with joy that she has borne well her part in the great song of creation!

Presently she returns to the camp, carrying the mysterious, the holy, the dearest bundle! She feels the endearing warmth of it and hears its soft breathing. It is still a part of herself, since both are nourished by the same mouthful, and no look of a lover could be sweeter than its deep, trusting gaze.

She continues her spiritual teaching, at first silently—a mere pointing of the index finger to nature; then in whispered songs, bird-like, at morning and evening. To her and to the child the birds are real people, who live very close to the "Great Mystery"; the murmuring trees breathe His presence; the falling waters chant His praise.

If the child should chance to be fretful, the mother raises her hand. "Hush! hush!" she cautions it tenderly, "the spirits may be disturbed!" She bids it be still and listen—listen to the silver voice of the aspen, or the clashing cymbals of the birch; and at night she points to the heavenly, blazed trail, through nature's galaxy of splendor to nature's God. Silence, love, reverence,—this is the trinity of first lessons; and to these she later adds generosity, courage, and chastity.

In the old days, our mothers were single-eyed to the trust imposed upon them; and as a noted chief of our people was wont to say: "Men may slay one another, but they can never overcome the woman, for in the quietude of her lap lies the child! You may destroy him once and again, but he issues as often from that same gentle lap—a gift of the Great Good to the race, in which man is only an accomplice!"

This wild mother has not only the experience of her mother and grandmother, and the accepted rules of her people for a guide, but she humbly seeks to learn a lesson from ants, bees, spiders, beavers, and badgers. She studies the family life of the birds, so exquisite in its emotional intensity and its patient devotion, until she seems to feel the universal mother-heart beating in her own breast. In due time the child takes of his own accord the attitude of prayer, and speaks reverently of the Powers. He thinks that he is a blood brother to all living creatures, and the storm wind is to him a messenger of the "Great Mystery."

At the age of about eight years, if he is a boy, she turns him over to his father for more Spartan training. If a girl, she is from this time much under the guardianship of her grandmother, who is considered the most dignified protector for the maiden. Indeed, the distinctive work of both grandparents is that of acquainting the youth with the national traditions and beliefs. It is reserved for them to repeat the time-hallowed tales with dignity and authority, so as to lead him into his inheritance in the stored-up wisdom and experience of the race. The old are dedicated to the service of the young, as their teachers and advisers, and the young in turn regard them with love and reverence.

Our old age was in some respects the happiest period of life. Advancing years brought with them much freedom, not only from the burden of laborious and dangerous tasks, but from those restrictions of custom and etiquette which were religiously observed by all others. No one who is at all acquainted with the Indian in his home can deny that we are a polite people. As a rule, the warrior who inspired the greatest terror in the hearts of his enemies was a man of the most exemplary gentleness, and almost feminine refinement, among his family and friends. A soft, low voice was considered an excellent thing in man, as well as in woman! Indeed, the enforced intimacy of tent life would soon become intolerable, were it not for these instinctive reserves and delicacies, this unfailing respect for the established place and possessions of every other member of the family circle, this habitual quiet, order, and decorum.

Our people, though capable of strong and durable feeling, were not demonstrative in their affection at any time, least of all in the presence of guests or strangers. Only to the aged, who have journeyed far, and are in a manner exempt from ordinary rules, are permitted some playful familiarities with children and grandchildren, some plain speaking, even to harshness and objurgation, from which the others must rigidly refrain. In short, the old men and women are privileged to say what they please and how they please, without contradiction, while the hardships and bodily infirmities that of necessity fall to their lot are softened so far as may be by universal consideration and attention.

There was no religious ceremony connected with marriage among us, while on the other hand the relation between man and woman was regarded as in itself mysterious and holy. It appears that where marriage is solemnized by the church and blessed by the priest, it may at the same time be surrounded with customs and ideas of a frivolous, superficial, and even prurient character. We believed that two who love should be united in secret, before the public acknowledgment of their union, and should taste their apotheosis alone with nature. The betrothal might or might not be discussed and approved by the parents, but in either case it was customary for the young pair to disappear into the wilderness, there to pass some days or weeks in perfect seclusion and dual solitude, afterward returning to the village as man and wife. An exchange of presents and entertainments between the two families usually followed, but the nuptial blessing was given by the High Priest of God, the most reverend and holy Nature.

The family was not only the social unit, but also the unit of government. The clan is nothing more than a larger family, with its patriarchal chief as the natural head, and the union of several clans by intermarriage and voluntary connection constitutes the tribe. The very name of our tribe, Dakota, means Allied People. The remoter degrees of kinship were fully recognized, and that not as a matter of form only: first cousins were known as brothers and sisters; the name of "cousin" constituted a binding claim, and our rigid morality forbade marriage between cousins in any known degree, or in other words within the clan.

The household proper consisted of a man with one or more wives and their children, all of whom dwelt amicably together, often under one roof, although some men of rank and position provided a separate lodge for each wife. There were, indeed, few plural marriages except among the older and leading men, and plural wives were usually, though not necessarily, sisters. A marriage might honorably be dissolved for cause, but there was very little infidelity or immorality, either open or secret.

It has been said that the position of woman is the test of civilization, and that of our women was secure. In them was vested our standard of morals and the purity of our blood. The wife did not take the name of her husband nor enter his clan, and the children belonged to the clan of the mother. All of the family property was held by her, descent was traced in the maternal line, and the honor of the house was in her hands. Modesty was her chief adornment; hence the younger women were usually silent and retiring: but a woman who had attained to ripeness of years and wisdom, or who had displayed notable courage in some emergency, was sometimes invited to a seat in the council.

Thus she ruled undisputed within her own domain, and was to us a tower of moral and spiritual strength, until the coming of the border white man, the soldier and trader, who with strong drink overthrew the honor of the man, and through his power over a worthless husband purchased the virtue of his wife or his daughter. When she fell, the whole race fell with her.

Before this calamity came upon us, you could not find anywhere a happier home than that created by the Indian woman. There was nothing of the artificial about her person, and very little disingenuousness in her character. Her early and consistent training, the definiteness of her vocation, and, above all, her profoundly religious attitude gave her a strength and poise that could not be overcome by any ordinary misfortune.

Indian names were either characteristic nicknames given in a playful spirit, deed names, birth names, or such as have a religious and symbolic meaning. It has been said that when a child is born, some accident or unusual appearance determines his name. This is sometimes the case, but is not the rule. A man of forcible character, with a fine war record, usually bears the name of the buffalo or bear, lightning or some dread natural force. Another of more peaceful nature may be called Swift Bird or Blue Sky. A woman's name usually suggested something about the home, often with the adjective "pretty" or "good," and a feminine termination. Names of any dignity or importance must be conferred by the old men, and especially so if they have any spiritual significance; as Sacred Cloud, Mysterious Night, Spirit Woman, and the like. Such a name was sometimes borne by three generations, but each individual must prove that he is worthy of it.

In the life of the Indian there was only one inevitable duty,—the duty of prayer—the daily recognition of the Unseen and Eternal. His daily devotions were more necessary to him than daily food. He wakes at daybreak, puts on his moccasins and steps down to the water's edge. Here he throws handfuls of clear, cold water into his face, or plunges in bodily. After the bath, he stands erect before the advancing dawn, facing the sun as it dances upon the horizon, and offers his unspoken orison. His mate may precede or follow him in his devotions, but never accompanies him. Each soul must meet the morning sun, the new, sweet earth, and the Great Silence alone!

Whenever, in the course of the daily hunt, the red hunter comes upon a scene that is strikingly beautiful or sublime—a black thundercloud with the rainbow's glowing arch above the mountain; a white waterfall in the heart of a green gorge; a vast prairie tinged with the blood-red of sunset—he pauses for an instant in the attitude of worship. He sees no need for setting apart one day in seven as a holy day, since to him all days are God's.

Every act of his life is, in a very real sense, a religious act. He recognizes the spirit in all creation, and believes that he draws from it spiritual power. His respect for the immortal part of the animal, his brother, often leads him so far as to lay out the body of his game in state and decorate the head with symbolic paint or feathers. Then he stands before it in the prayer attitude, holding up the filled pipe, in token that he has freed with honor the spirit of his brother, whose body his need compelled him to take to sustain his own life.

When food is taken, the woman murmurs a "grace" as she lowers the kettle; an act so softly and unobtrusively performed that one who does not know the custom usually fails to catch the whisper: "Spirit, partake!" As her husband receives the bowl or plate, he likewise murmurs his invocation to the spirit. When he becomes an old man, he loves to make a notable effort to prove his gratitude. He cuts off the choicest morsel of the meat and casts it into the fire—the purest and most ethereal element.

The hospitality of the wigwam is only limited by the institution of war. Yet, if an enemy should honor us with a call, his trust will not be misplaced, and he will go away convinced that he has met with a royal host! Our honor is the guarantee for his safety, so long as he is within the camp.

Friendship is held to be the severest test of character. It is easy, we think, to be loyal to family and clan, whose blood is in our own veins. Love between man and woman is founded on the mating instinct and is not free from desire and self-seeking. But to have a friend, and to be true under any and all trials, is the mark of a man!

The highest type of friendship is the relation of "brother-friend" or "life-and-death friend." This bond is between man and man, is usually formed in early youth, and can only be broken by death. It is the essence of comradeship and fraternal love, without thought of pleasure or gain, but rather for moral support and inspiration. Each is vowed to die for the other, if need be, and nothing is denied the brother-friend, but neither is anything required that is not in accord with the highest conceptions of the Indian mind.

III

CEREMONIAL AND SYMBOLIC WORSHIP

Modern Perversions of Early Religious Rites.
The Sun Dance. The Great Medicine Lodge.
Totems and Charms. The Vapor-Bath
and the Ceremonial of the Pipe.

The public religious rites of the Plains Indians are few, and in large part of modern origin, belonging properly to the so-called "transition period." That period must be held to begin with the first insidious effect upon their manners and customs of contact with the dominant race, and many of the tribes were so influenced long before they ceased to lead the nomadic life.

The fur-traders, the "Black Robe" priests, the military, and finally the Protestant missionaries, were the men who began the disintegration of the Indian nations and the overthrow of their religion, seventy-five to a hundred years before they were forced to enter upon reservation life. We have no authentic study of them until well along in the transition period, when whiskey and trade had already debauched their native ideals.

During the era of reconstruction they modified their customs and beliefs continually, creating a singular admixture of Christian with pagan superstitions, and an addition to the old folk-lore of disguised Bible stories under an Indian aspect. Even their music shows the influence of the Catholic chants. Most of the material collected by modern observers is necessarily of this promiscuous character.

It is noteworthy that the first effect of contact with the whites was an increase of cruelty and barbarity, an intensifying of the dark shadows in the picture! In this manner the "Sun Dance" of the Plains Indians, the most important of their public ceremonials, was abused and perverted until it became a horrible exhibition of barbarism, and was eventually prohibited by the Government.

In the old days, when a Sioux warrior found himself in the very jaws of destruction, he might offer a prayer to his father, the Sun, to prolong his life. If rescued from imminent danger, he must acknowledge the divine favor by making a Sun Dance, according to the vow embraced in his prayer, in which he declared that he did not fear torture or death, but asked life only for the sake of those who loved him. Thus the physical ordeal was the fulfillment of a vow, and a sort of atonement for what might otherwise appear to be reprehensible weakness in the face of death. It was in the nature of confession and thank-offering to the "Great Mystery," through the physical parent, the Sun, and did not embrace a prayer for future favors.

The ceremonies usually took place from six months to a year after the making of the vow, in order to admit of suitable preparation; always in midsummer and before a large and imposing gathering. They naturally included the making of a feast, and the giving away of much savage wealth in honor of the occasion, although these were no essential part of the religious rite.

When the day came to procure the pole, it was brought in by a party of warriors, headed by some man of distinction. The tree selected was six to eight inches in diameter at the base, and twenty to twenty-five feet high. It was chosen and felled with some solemnity, including the ceremony of the "filled pipe," and was carried in the fashion of a litter, symbolizing the body of the man who made the dance. A solitary teepee was pitched on a level spot at some distance from the village, and the pole raised near at hand with the same ceremony, in the centre of a circular enclosure of fresh-cut boughs.

Meanwhile, one of the most noted of our old men had carved out of rawhide, or later of wood, two figures, usually those of a man and a buffalo. Sometimes the figure of a bird, supposed to represent the Thunder, was substituted for the buffalo. It was customary to paint the man red and the animal black, and each was suspended from one end of the crossbar which was securely tied some two feet from the top of the pole. I have never been able to determine that this cross had any significance; it was probably nothing more than a dramatic coincidence that surmounted the Sun-Dance pole with the symbol of Christianity.

The paint indicated that the man who was about to give thanks publicly had been potentially dead, but was allowed to live by the mysterious favor and interference of the Giver of Life. The buffalo hung opposite the image of his own body in death, because it was the support of his physical self, and a leading figure in legendary lore. Following the same line of thought, when he emerged from the solitary lodge of preparation, and approached the pole to dance, nude save for his breechclout and moccasins, his hair loosened and daubed with clay, he must drag after him a buffalo skull, representing the grave from which he had escaped.

The dancer was cut or scarified on the chest, sufficient to draw blood and cause pain, the natural accompaniments of his figurative death. He took his position opposite the singers, facing the pole, and dragging the skull by leather thongs which were merely fastened about his shoulders. During a later period, incisions were made in the breast or back, sometimes both, through which wooden skewers were drawn, and secured by lariats to the pole or to the skulls. Thus he danced without intermission for a day and a night, or even longer, ever gazing at the sun in the daytime, and blowing from time to time a sacred whistle made from the bone of a goose's wing.

In recent times, this rite was exaggerated and distorted into a mere ghastly display of physical strength and endurance under torture, almost on a level with the Caucasian institution of the bull-fight, or the yet more modern prize-ring. Moreover, instead of an atonement or thank-offering, it became the accompaniment of a prayer for success in war, or in a raid upon the horses of the enemy. The number of dancers was increased, and they were made to hang suspended from the pole by their own flesh, which they must break loose before being released. I well remember the comments in our own home upon the passing of this simple but impressive ceremony, and its loss of all meaning and propriety under the demoralizing additions which were some of the fruits of early contact with the white man.

Perhaps the most remarkable organization ever known among American Indians, that of the "Grand Medicine Lodge," was apparently an indirect result of the labors of the early Jesuit missionaries. In it Caucasian ideas are easily recognizable, and it seems reasonable to suppose that its founders desired to establish an order that would successfully resist the encroachments of the "Black Robes." However that may be, it is an unquestionable fact that the only religious leaders of any note who have arisen among the native tribes since the advent of the white man, the "Shawnee Prophet" in 1762, and the half breed prophet of the "Ghost Dance" in 1890, both founded their claims or prophecies upon the Gospel story. Thus in each case an Indian religious revival or craze, though more or less threatening to the invader, was of distinctively alien origin.

The Medicine Lodge originated among the Algonquin tribe, and extended gradually throughout its branches, finally affecting the Sioux of the Mississippi Valley, and forming a strong bulwark against the work of the pioneer missionaries, who secured, indeed, scarcely any converts until after the outbreak of 1862, when subjection, starvation, and imprison-ment turned our broken-hearted people to accept Christianity, which seemed to offer them the only gleam of kindness or hope.

The order was a secret one, and in some respects not unlike the Free Masons, being a union or affiliation of a number of lodges, each with its distinctive songs and medicines. Leadership was in order of seniority in degrees, which could only be obtained by merit, and women were admitted to membership upon equal terms, with the possibility of attaining to the highest honors. No person might become a member unless his moral standing was excellent, all candidates remained on probation for one or two years, and murderers and adulterers were expelled. The commandments promulgated by this order were essentially the same as the Mosaic Ten, so that it exerted a distinct moral influence, in addition to its ostensible object, which was instruction in the secrets of legitimate medicine.

In this society the uses of all curative roots and herbs known to us were taught exhaustively and practiced mainly by the old, the younger members being in training to fill the places of those who passed away. My grandmother was a well-known and successful practitioner, and both my mother and father were members, but did not practice.

A medicine or "mystery feast" was not a public affair, as members only were eligible, and upon these occasions all the "medicine bags" and totems of the various lodges were displayed and their peculiar "medicine songs" were sung. The food was only partaken of by invited guests, and not by the hosts, or lodge making the feast.

The "Grand Medicine Dance" was given on the occasion of initiating those candidates who had finished their probation, a sufficient number of whom were designated to take the places of those who had died since the last meeting. Invitations were sent out in the form of small bundles of tobacco. Two very large teepees were pitched facing one another, a hundred feet apart, half open, and connected by a roofless hall or colonnade of fresh-cut boughs. One of these lodges was for the society giving the dance and the novices, the other was occupied by the "soldiers," whose duty it was to distribute the refreshments, and to keep order among the spectators. They were selected from among the best and bravest warriors of the tribe.

The preparations being complete, and the members of each lodge garbed and painted according to their rituals, they entered the hall separately, in single file, led by their oldest man or "Great Chief." Standing before the "Soldiers' Lodge," facing the setting sun, their chief addressed the "Great Mystery" directly in a few words, after which all extending the right arm horizontally from the shoulder with open palm, sang a short invocation in unison, ending with a deep: "E-ho-ho-ho!" This performance, which was really impressive, was repeated in front of the headquarters lodge, facing the rising sun, after which each lodge took its assigned place, and the songs and dances followed in regular order.

The closing ceremony, which was intensely dramatic in its character, was the initiation of the novices, who had received their final preparation on the night before. They were now led out in front of the headquarters lodge and placed in a kneeling position upon a carpet of rich robes and furs, the men upon the right hand, stripped and painted black, with a round spot of red just over the heart, while the women, dressed in their best, were arranged upon the left. Both sexes wore the hair loose, as if in mourning or expectation of death. An equal number of grand medicine-men, each of whom was especially appointed to one of the novices, faced them at a distance of half the length of the hall, or perhaps fifty feet.

After silent prayer, each medicine-man in turn addressed himself to his charge, exhorting him to observe all the rules of the order under the eye of the Mysterious One, and instructing him in his duty toward his fellow-man and toward the Ruler of Life. All then assumed an attitude of superb power and dignity, crouching slightly as if about to spring forward in a foot-race, and grasping their medicine bags firmly in both hands. Swinging their arms forward at the same moment, they uttered their guttural "Yo-ho-ho-ho!" in perfect unison and with startling effect. In the midst of a breathless silence, they took a step forward, then another and another, ending a rod or so from the row of kneeling victims, with a mighty swing of the sacred bags that would seem to project all their mystic power into the bodies of the initiates. Instantly they all fell forward, apparently lifeless.

With this thrilling climax, the drums were vigorously pounded and the dance began again with energy. After a few turns had been taken about the prostrate bodies of the new members, covering them with fine robes and other garments which were later to be distributed as gifts, they were permitted to come to life and to join in the final dance. The whole performance was clearly symbolic of death and resurrection.

While I cannot suppose that this elaborate ritual, with its use of public and audible prayer, of public exhortation or sermon, and other Caucasian features, was practiced before comparatively modern times, there is no doubt that it was conscientiously believed in by its members, and for a time regarded with reverence by the people. But at a later period it became still further demoralized and fell under suspicion of witchcraft.

There is no doubt that the Indian held medicine close to spiritual things, but in this also he has been much misunderstood; in fact everything that he held sacred is indiscriminately called "medicine," in the sense of mystery or magic. As a doctor he was originally very adroit and often successful. He employed only healing bark, roots, and leaves with whose properties he was familiar, using them in the form of a distillation or tea and always singly. The stomach or internal bath was a valuable discovery of his, and the vapor or Turkish bath was in general use. He could set a broken bone with fair success, but never practiced surgery in any form. In addition to all this, the medicine-man possessed much personal magnetism and authority, and in his treatment often sought to reestablish the equilibrium of the patient through mental or spiritual influences—a sort of primitive psychotherapy.

The Sioux word for the healing art is "wah-pee-yah," which literally means readjusting or making anew. "Pay-jee-hoo-tah," literally root, means medicine, and "wakan" signifies spirit or mystery. Thus the three ideas, while sometimes associated, were carefully distinguished.

It is important to remember that in the old days the "medicine-man" received no payment for his services, which were of the nature of an honorable function or office. When the idea of payment and barter was introduced among us, and valuable presents or fees began to be demanded for treating the sick, the ensuing greed and rivalry led to many demoralizing practices, and in time to the rise of the modern "conjurer," who is generally a fraud and trickster of the grossest kind. It is fortunate that his day is practically over.

Ever seeking to establish spiritual comradeship with the animal creation, the Indian adopted this or that animal as his "totem," the emblematic device of his society, family, or clan. It is probable that the creature chosen was the traditional ancestress, as we are told that the First Man had many wives among the animal people. The sacred beast, bird, or reptile, represented by its stuffed skin, or by a rude painting, was treated with reverence and carried into battle to insure the guardianship of the spirits. The symbolic attribute of beaver, bear, or tortoise, such as wisdom, cunning, courage, and the like, was supposed to be mysteriously conferred upon the wearer of the badge. The totem or charm used in medicine was ordinarily that of the medicine lodge to which the practitioner belonged, though there were some great men who boasted a special revelation.

There are two ceremonial usages which, so far as I have been able to ascertain, were universal among American Indians, and apparently fundamental. These have already been referred to as the "eneepee," or vapor-bath, and the "chan-du-hu-pah-yu-za-pee," or ceremonial of the pipe. In our Siouan legends and traditions these two are preeminent, as handed down from the most ancient time and persisting to the last.

In our Creation myth or story of the First Man, the vapor-bath was the magic used by The-one-who-was-First-Created, to give life to the dead bones of his younger brother, who had been slain by the monsters of the deep. Upon the shore of the Great Water he dug two round holes, over one of which he built a low enclosure of fragrant cedar boughs, and here he gathered together the bones of his brother. In the other pit he made a fire and heated four round stones, which he rolled one by one into the lodge of boughs. Having closed every aperture save one, he sang a mystic chant while he thrust in his arm and sprinkled water upon the stones with a bunch of sage. Immediately steam arose, and as the legend says, "there was an appearance of life." A second time he sprinkled water, and the dry bones rattled together. The third time he seemed to hear soft singing from within the lodge; and the fourth time a voice exclaimed: "Brother, let me out!" (It should be noted that the number four is the magic or sacred number of the Indian.)

This story gives the traditional origin of the "eneepee," which has ever since been deemed essential to the Indian's effort to purify and recreate his spirit. It is used both by the doctor and by his patient. Every man must enter the cleansing bath and take the cold plunge which follows, when preparing for any spiritual crisis, for possible death, or imminent danger.

Not only the "eneepee" itself, but everything used in connection with the mysterious event, the aromatic cedar and sage, the water, and especially the water-worn boulders, are regarded as sacred, or at the least adapted to a spiritual use. For the rock we have a special reverent name—"Tunkan," a contraction of the Sioux word for Grandfather.

The natural boulder enters into many of our solemn ceremonials, such as the "Rain Dance," and the "Feast of Virgins." The lone hunter and warrior reverently holds up his filled pipe to "Tunkan," in solitary commemoration of a miracle which to him is as authentic and holy as the raising of Lazarus to the devout Christian.

There is a legend that the First Man fell sick, and was taught by his Elder Brother the ceremonial use of the pipe, in a prayer to the spirits for ease and relief. This simple ceremony is the commonest daily expression of thanks or "grace," as well as an oath of loyalty and good faith when the warrior goes forth upon some perilous enterprise, and it enters even into his "hambeday," or solitary prayer, ascending as a rising vapor or incense to the Father of Spirits.

In all the war ceremonies and in medicine a special pipe is used, but at home or on the hunt the warrior employs his own. The pulverized weed is mixed with aromatic bark of the red willow, and pressed lightly into the bowl of the long stone pipe. The worshiper lights it gravely and takes a whiff or two; then, standing erect, he holds it silently toward the Sun, our father, and toward the earth, our mother. There are modern variations, as holding the pipe to the Four Winds, the Fire, Water, Rock, and other elements or objects of reverence.

There are many religious festivals which are local and special in character, embodying a prayer for success in hunting or warfare, or for rain and bountiful harvests, but these two are the sacraments of our religion. For baptism we substitute the "eneepee," the purification by vapor, and in our holy communion we partake of the soothing incense of tobacco in the stead of bread and wine.

IV

BARBARISM AND THE MORAL CODE

Silence the Corner-Stone of Character. Basic Ideas of Morality. "Give All or Nothing!" Rules of Honorable Warfare. An Indian Conception of Courage.

Long before I ever heard of Christ, or saw a white man, I had learned from an untutored woman the essence of morality. With the help of dear Nature herself, she taught me things simple but of mighty import. I knew God. I perceived what goodness is. I saw and loved what is really beautiful. Civilization has not taught me anything better!

As a child, I understood how to give; I have forgotten that grace since I became civilized. I lived the natural life, whereas I now live the artificial. Any pretty pebble was valuable to me then; every growing tree an object of reverence. Now I worship with the white man before a painted landscape whose value is estimated in dollars! Thus the Indian is reconstructed, as the natural rocks are ground to powder, and made into artificial blocks which may be built into the walls of modern society.

The first American mingled with his pride a singular humility. Spiritual arrogance was foreign to his nature and teaching. He never claimed that the power of articulate speech was proof of superiority over the dumb creation; on the other hand, it is to him a perilous gift. He believes profoundly in silence—the sign of a perfect equilibrium. Silence is the absolute poise or balance of body, mind, and spirit. The man who preserves his selfhood ever calm and unshaken by the storms of existence—not a leaf, as it were, astir on the tree; not a ripple upon the surface of shining pool—his, in the mind of the unlettered sage, is the ideal attitude and conduct of life.

If you ask him: "What is silence?" he will answer: "It is the Great Mystery!" "The holy silence is His voice!" If you ask: "What are the fruits of silence?" he will say: "They are self-control, true courage or endurance, patience, dignity, and reverence. Silence is the cornerstone of character."

"Guard your tongue in youth," said the old chief, Wabashaw, "and in age you may mature a thought that will be of service to your people!"

The moment that man conceived of a perfect body, supple, symmetrical, graceful, and enduring—in that moment he had laid the foundation of a moral life! No man can hope to maintain such a temple of the spirit beyond the period of adolescence, unless he is able to curb his indulgence in the pleasures of the senses. Upon this truth the Indian built a rigid system of physical training, a social and moral code that was the law of his life.

There was aroused in him as a child a high ideal of manly strength and beauty, the attainment of which must depend upon strict temperance in eating and in the sexual relation, together with severe and persistent exercise. He desired to be a worthy link in the generations, and that he might not destroy by his weakness that vigor and purity of blood which had been achieved at the cost of much self-denial by a long line of ancestors.

He was required to fast from time to time for short periods, and to work off his superfluous energy by means of hard running, swimming, and the vapor-bath. The bodily fatigue thus induced, especially when coupled with a reduced diet, is a reliable cure for undue sexual desires.

Personal modesty was early cultivated as a safeguard, together with a strong self-respect and pride of family and race. This was accomplished in part by keeping the child ever before the public eye, from his birth onward. His entrance into the world, especially in the case of the first-born, was often publicly announced by the herald, accompanied by a distribution of presents to the old and needy. The same thing occurred when he took his first step, when his ears were pierced, and when he shot his first game, so that his childish exploits and progress were known to the whole clan as to a larger family, and he grew into manhood with the saving sense of a reputation to sustain.

The youth was encouraged to enlist early in the public service, and to develop a wholesome ambition for the honors of a leader and feast-maker, which can never be his unless he is truthful and generous, as well as brave, and ever mindful of his personal chastity and honor. There were many ceremonial customs which had a distinct moral influence; the woman was rigidly secluded at certain periods, and the young husband was forbidden to approach his own wife when preparing for war or for any religious event. The public or tribal position of the Indian is entirely dependent upon his private virtue, and he is never permitted to forget that he does not live to himself alone, but to his tribe and his clan. Thus habits of perfect self-control were early established, and there were no unnatural conditions or complex temptations to beset him until he was met and overthrown by a stronger race.

To keep the young men and young women strictly to their honor, there were observed among us, within my own recollection, certain annual ceremonies of a semi-religious nature. One of the most impressive of these was the sacred "Feast of Virgins," which, when given for the first time, was equivalent to the public announcement of a young girl's arrival at a marriageable age. The herald, making the rounds of the teepee village, would publish the feast something after this fashion:

"Pretty Weasel-woman, the daughter of Brave Bear, will kindle her first maidens' fire to-morrow! All ye who have never yielded to the pleading of man, who have not destroyed your innocency, you alone are invited, to proclaim anew before the Sun and the Earth, before your companions and in the sight of the Great Mystery, the chastity and purity of your maidenhood. Come ye, all who have not known man!"

The whole village was at once aroused to the interest of the coming event, which was considered next to the Sun Dance and the Grand Medicine Dance in public importance. It always took place in midsummer, when a number of different clans were gathered together for the summer festivities, and was held in the centre of the great circular encampment.

Here two circles were described, one within the other, about a rudely heart-shaped rock which was touched with red paint, and upon either side of the rock there were thrust into the ground a knife and two arrows. The inner circle was for the maidens, and the outer one for their grandmothers or chaperones, who were supposed to have passed the climacteric. Upon the outskirts of the feast there was a great public gathering, in which order was kept by certain warriors of highest reputation. Any man among the spectators might approach and challenge any young woman whom he knew to be unworthy; but if the accuser failed to prove his charge, the warriors were accustomed to punish him severely.

Each girl in turn approached the sacred rock and laid her hand upon it with all solemnity. This was her religious declaration of her virginity, her vow to remain pure until her marriage. If she should ever violate the maidens' oath, then welcome that keen knife and those sharp arrows!

Our maidens were ambitious to attend a number of these feasts before marriage, and it sometimes happened that a girl was compelled to give one, on account of gossip about her conduct. Then it was in the nature of a challenge to the scandalmongers to prove their words! A similar feast was sometimes made by the young men, for whom the rules were even more strict, since no young man might attend this feast who had so much as spoken of love to a maiden. It was considered a high honor among us to have won some distinction in war and the chase, and above all to have been invited to a seat in the council, before one had spoken to any girl save his own sister.

It was our belief that the love of possessions is a weakness to be overcome. Its appeal is to the material part, and if allowed its way it will in time disturb the spiritual balance of the man. Therefore the child must early learn the beauty of generosity. He is taught to give what he prizes most, and that he may taste the happiness of giving, he is made at an early age the family almoner. If a child is inclined to be grasping, or to cling to any of his little possessions, legends are related to him, telling of the contempt and disgrace falling upon the ungenerous and mean man.

Public giving is a part of every important ceremony. It properly belongs to the celebration of birth, marriage, and death, and is observed whenever it is desired to do special honor to any person or event. Upon such occasions it is common to give to the point of utter impoverishment. The Indian in his simplicity literally gives away all that he has, to relatives, to guests of another tribe or clan, but above all to the poor and the aged, from whom he can hope for no return. Finally, the gift to the "Great Mystery," the religious offering, may be of little value in itself, but to the giver's own thought it should carry the meaning and reward of true sacrifice.

Orphans and the aged are invariably cared for, not only by their next of kin, but by the whole clan. It is the loving parent's pride to have his daughters visit the unfortunate and the helpless, carry them food, comb their hair, and mend their garments. The name "Wenonah," bestowed upon the eldest daughter, distinctly implies all this, and a girl who failed in her charitable duties was held to be unworthy of the name.

The man who is a skillful hunter, and whose wife is alive to her opportunities, makes many feasts, to which he is careful to invite the older men of his clan, recognizing that they have outlived their period of greatest activity, and now love nothing so well as to eat in good company, and to live over the past. The old men, for their part, do their best to requite his liberality with a little speech, in which they are apt to relate the brave and generous deeds of their host's ancestors, finally congratulating him upon being a worthy successor of an honorable line. Thus his reputation is won as a hunter and a feast-maker, and almost as famous in his way as the great warrior is he who has a recognized name and standing as a "man of peace."

The true Indian sets no price upon either his property or his labor. His generosity is only limited by his strength and ability. He regards it as an honor to be selected for a difficult or dangerous service, and would think it shame to ask for any reward, saying rather: "Let him whom I serve express his thanks according to his own bringing up and his sense of honor!"

Nevertheless, he recognizes rights in property. To steal from one of his own tribe would be indeed disgrace, and if discovered, the name of "Wamanon," or Thief, is fixed upon him forever as an unalterable stigma. The only exception to the rule is in the case of food, which is always free to the hungry if there is none by to offer it. Other protection than the moral law there could not be in an Indian community, where there were neither locks nor doors, and everything was open and easy of access to all comers.

The property of the enemy is spoil of war, and it is always allowable to confiscate it if possible. However, in the old days there was not much plunder. Before the coming of the white man, there was in fact little temptation or opportunity to despoil the enemy; but in modern times the practice of "stealing horses" from hostile tribes has become common, and is thought far from dishonorable.

Warfare we regarded as an institution of the "Great Mystery"— an organized tournament or trial of courage and skill, with elaborate rules and "counts" for the coveted honor of the eagle feather. It was held to develop the quality of manliness and its motive was chivalric or patriotic, but never the desire for territorial aggrandizement or the overthrow of a brother nation.

It was common, in early times, for a battle or skirmish to last all day, with great display of daring and horsemanship, but with scarcely more killed and wounded than may be carried from the field during a university game of football.

The slayer of a man in battle was expected to mourn for thirty days blackening his face and loosening his hair according to the custom. He of course considered it no sin to take the life of an enemy, and this ceremonial mourning was a sign of reverence for the departed spirit. The killing in war of non-combatants, such as women and children, is partly explained by the fact that in savage life the woman without husband or protector is in pitiable case, and it was supposed that the spirit of the warrior would be better content if no widow and orphans were left to suffer want, as well as to weep.

A scalp might originally be taken by the leader of the war party only and at that period no other mutilation was practiced. It was a small lock not more than three inches square, which was carried only during the thirty days' celebration of a victory, and afterward given religious burial. Wanton cruelties and the more barbarous customs of war were greatly intensified with the coming of the white man, who brought with him fiery liquor and deadly weapons, aroused the Indian's worst passions, provoking in him revenge and cupidity, and even offered bounties for the scalps of innocent men, women, and children.

Murder within the tribe was a grave offense, to be atoned for as the council might decree, and it often happened that the slayer was called upon to pay the penalty with his own life. He made no attempt to escape or to evade justice. That the crime was committed in the depths of the forest or at dead of night, witnessed by no human eye, made no difference to his mind. He was thoroughly convinced that all is known to the "Great Mystery," and hence did not hesitate to give himself up, to stand his trial by the old and wise men of the victim's clan. His own family and clan might by no means attempt to excuse or to defend him, but his judges took all the known circumstances into consideration, and if it appeared that he slew in self-defense, or that the provocation was severe, he might be set free after a thirty days' period of mourning in solitude. Otherwise the murdered man's next of kin were authorized to take his life; and if they refrained from doing so, as often happened, he remained an outcast from the clan. A willful murder was a rare occurrence before the days of whiskey and drunken rows, for we were not a violent or a quarrelsome people.

It is well remembered that Crow Dog, who killed the Sioux chief, Spotted Tail, in 1881, calmly surrendered himself and was tried and convicted by the courts in South Dakota. After his conviction, he was permitted remarkable liberty in prison, such as perhaps no white man has ever enjoyed when under sentence of death.

The cause of his act was a solemn commission received from his people, nearly thirty years earlier, at the time that Spotted Tail usurped the chieftainship by the aid of the military, whom he had aided. Crow Dog was under a vow to slay the chief, in case he ever betrayed or disgraced the name of the Brule Sioux. There is no doubt that he had committed crimes both public and private, having been guilty of misuse of office as well as of gross offenses against morality; therefore his death was not a matter of personal vengeance but of just retribution.

A few days before Crow Dog was to be executed, he asked permission to visit his home and say farewell to his wife and twin boys, then nine or ten years old. Strange to say, the request was granted, and the condemned man sent home under escort of the deputy sheriff, who remained at the Indian agency, merely telling his prisoner to report there on the following day. When he did not appear at the time set, the sheriff dispatched the Indian police after him. They did not find him, and his wife simply said that Crow Dog had desired to ride alone to the prison, and would reach there on the day appointed.

All doubt was removed next day by a telegram from Rapid City, two hundred miles distant, saying: "Crow Dog has just reported here."

The incident drew public attention to the Indian murderer, with the unexpected result that the case was reopened, and Crow Dog acquitted. He still lives, a well-preserved man of about seventy-five years, and is much respected among his own people.

It is said that, in the very early days, lying was a capital offense among us. Believing that the deliberate liar is capable of committing any crime behind the screen of cowardly untruth and double-dealing, the destroyer of mutual confidence was summarily put to death, that the evil might go no further.

Even the worst enemies of the Indian, those who accuse him of treachery, blood-thirstiness, cruelty, and lust, have not denied his courage, but in their minds it is a courage that is ignorant, brutal, and fantastic. His own conception of bravery makes of it a high moral virtue, for to him it consists not so much in aggressive self-assertion as in absolute self-control. The truly brave man, we contend, yields neither to fear nor anger, desire nor agony; he is at all times master of himself; his courage rises to the heights of chivalry, patriotism, and real heroism.

"Let neither cold, hunger, nor pain, nor the fear of them, neither the bristling teeth of danger nor the very jaws of death itself, prevent you from doing a good deed," said an old chief to a scout who was about to seek the buffalo in midwinter for the relief of a starving people. This was his childlike conception of courage.

V

THE UNWRITTEN SCRIPTURES

A Living Book. The Sioux Story of Creation. The First Battle. Another Version of the Flood. Our Animal Ancestry.

A missionary once undertook to instruct a group of Indians in the truths of his holy religion. He told them of the creation of the earth in six days, and of the fall of our first parents by eating an apple.

The courteous savages listened attentively, and, after thanking him, one related in his turn a very ancient tradition concerning the origin of the maize. But the missionary plainly showed his disgust and disbelief, indignantly saying:—

"What I delivered to you were sacred truths, but this that you tell me is mere fable and falsehood!"

"My brother," gravely replied the offended Indian, "it seems that you have not been well grounded in the rules of civility. You saw that we, who practice these rules, believed your stories; why, then, do you refuse to credit ours?"

Every religion has its Holy Book, and ours was a mingling of history, poetry, and prophecy, of precept and folk-lore, even such as the modern reader finds within the covers of his Bible. This Bible of ours was our whole literature, a living Book, sowed as precious seed by our wisest sages, and springing anew in the wondering eyes and upon the innocent lips of little children. Upon its hoary wisdom of proverb and fable, its mystic and legendary lore thus sacredly preserved and transmitted from father to son, was based in large part our customs and philosophy.

Naturally magnanimous and open-minded, the red man prefers to believe that the Spirit of God is not breathed into man alone, but that the whole created universe is a sharer in the immortal perfection of its Maker. His imaginative and poetic mind, like that of the Greek, assigns to every mountain, tree, and spring its spirit, nymph, or divinity either beneficent or mischievous.

The heroes and demigods of Indian tradition reflect the characteristic trend of his thought, and his attribution of personality and will to the elements, the sun and stars, and all animate or inanimate nature.

In the Sioux story of creation, the great Mysterious One is not brought directly upon the scene or conceived in anthropomorphic fashion, but remains sublimely in the background. The Sun and the Earth, representing the male and female principles, are the main elements in his creation, the other planets being subsidiary. The enkindling warmth of the Sun entered into the bosom of our mother, the Earth, and forthwith she conceived and brought forth life, both vegetable and animal.

Finally there appeared mysteriously Ish-na-e-cha-ge, the "First-Born," a being in the likeness of man, yet more than man, who roamed solitary among the animal people and understood their ways and their language. They beheld him with wonder and awe, for they could do nothing without his knowledge. He had pitched his tent in the centre of the land, and there was no spot impossible for him to penetrate.

At last, like Adam, the "First-Born" of the Sioux became weary of living alone, and formed for himself a companion—not a mate, but a brother—not out of a rib from his side, but from a splinter which he drew from his great toe! This was the Little Boy Man, who was not created full-grown, but as an innocent child, trusting and helpless. His Elder Brother was his teacher throughout every stage of human progress from infancy to manhood, and it is to the rules which he laid down, and his counsels to the Little Boy Man, that we trace many of our most deep-rooted beliefs and most sacred customs.

Foremost among the animal people was Unk-to-mee, the Spider, the original trouble-maker, who noted keenly the growth of the boy in wit and ingenuity, and presently advised the animals to make an end of him; "for," said he, "if you do not, some day he will be the master of us all!" But they all loved the Little Boy Man because he was so friendly and so playful. Only the monsters of the deep sea listened, and presently took his life, hiding his body in the bottom of the sea. Nevertheless, by the magic power of the First-Born, the body was recovered and was given life again in the sacred vapor-bath, as described in a former chapter.

Once more our first ancestor roamed happily among the animal people, who were in those days a powerful nation. He learned their ways and their language—for they had a common tongue in those days; learned to sing like the birds, to swim like the fishes, and to climb sure-footed over rocks like the mountain sheep. Notwithstanding that he was their good comrade and did them no harm, Unk-to-mee once more sowed dissension among the animals, and messages were sent into all quarters of the earth, sea, and air, that all the tribes might unite to declare war upon the solitary man who was destined to become their master.

After a time the young man discovered the plot, and came home very sorrowful. He loved his animal friends, and was grieved that they should combine against him. Besides, he was naked and unarmed. But his Elder Brother armed him with a bow and flint-headed arrows, a stone war-club and a spear. He likewise tossed a pebble four times into the air, and each time it became a cliff or wall of rock about the teepee.

"Now," said he, "it is time to fight and to assert your supremacy, for it is they who have brought the trouble upon you, and not you upon them!"

Night and day the Little Boy Man remained upon the watch for his enemies from the top of the wall, and at last he beheld the prairies black with buffalo herds, and the elk gathering upon the edges of the forest. Bears and wolves were closing in from all directions, and now from the sky the Thunder gave his fearful war-whoop, answered by the wolf's long howl.

The badgers and other burrowers began at once to undermine his rocky fortress, while the climbers undertook to scale its perpendicular walls.

Then for the first time on earth the bow was strung, and hundreds of flint-headed arrows found their mark in the bodies of the animals, while each time that the Boy Man swung his stone war-club, his enemies fell in countless numbers.

Finally the insects, the little people of the air, attacked him in a body, filling his eyes and ears, and tormenting him with their poisoned spears, so that he was in despair. He called for help upon his Elder Brother, who ordered him to strike the rocks with his stone war-club. As soon as he had done so, sparks of fire flew upon the dry grass of the prairie and it burst into flame. A mighty smoke ascended, which drove away the teasing swarms of the insect people, while the flames terrified and scattered the others.

This was the first dividing of the trail between man and the animal people, and when the animals had sued for peace, the treaty provided that they must ever after furnish man with flesh for his food and skins for clothing, though not without effort and danger on his part. The little insects refused to make any concession, and have ever since been the tormentors of man; however, the birds of the air declared that they would punish them for their obstinacy, and this they continue to do unto this day.

Our people have always claimed that the stone arrows which are found so generally throughout the country are the ones that the first man used in his battle with the animals. It is not recorded in our traditions, much less is it within the memory of our old men, that we have ever made or used similar arrow-heads. Some have tried to make use of them for shooting fish under water, but with little success, and they are absolutely useless with the Indian bow which was in use when America was discovered. It is possible that they were made by some pre-historic race who used much longer and stronger bows, and who were workers in stone, which our people were not. Their stone implements were merely natural boulders or flint chips, fitted with handles of raw-hide or wood, except the pipes, which were carved from a species of stone which is soft when first quarried, and therefore easily worked with the most primitive tools. Practically all the flint arrow-heads that we see in museums and elsewhere were picked up or ploughed up, while some have been dishonestly sold by trafficking Indians and others, embedded in trees and bones.

We had neither devil nor hell in our religion until the white man brought them to us, yet Unk-to-mee, the Spider, was doubtless akin to that old Serpent who tempted mother Eve. He is always characterized as tricky, treacherous, and at the same time affable and charming, being not without the gifts of wit, prophecy, and eloquence. He is an adroit magician, able to assume almost any form at will, and impervious to any amount of ridicule and insult. Here we have, it appears, the elements of the story in Genesis; the primal Eden, the tempter in animal form, and the bringing of sorrow and death upon earth through the elemental sins of envy and jealousy.

The warning conveyed in the story of Unk-to-mee was ever used with success by Indian parents, and especially grandparents, in the instruction of their children. Ish-na-e-cha-ge, on the other hand, was a demigod and mysterious teacher, whose function it was to initiate the first man into his tasks and pleasures here on earth.

After the battle with the animals, there followed a battle with the elements, which in some measure parallels the Old Testament story of the flood. In this case, the purpose seems to have been to destroy the wicked animal people, who were too many and too strong for the lone man.

The legend tells us that when fall came, the First-Born advised his younger brother to make for himself a warm tent of buffalo skins, and to store up much food. No sooner had he done this than it began to snow, and the snow fell steadily during many moons. The Little Boy Man made for himself snow-shoes, and was thus enabled to hunt easily, while the animals fled from him with difficulty. Finally wolves, foxes, and ravens came to his door to beg for food, and he helped them, but many of the fiercer wild animals died of cold and starvation.

One day, when the hungry ones appeared, the snow was higher than the tops of the teepee poles, but the Little Boy Man's fire kept a hole open and clear. Down this hole they peered, and lo! the man had rubbed ashes on his face by the advice of his Elder Brother, and they both lay silent and motionless on either side of the fire.

Then the fox barked and the raven cawed his signal to the wandering tribes, and they all rejoiced and said: "Now they are both dying or dead, and we shall have no more trouble!" But the sun appeared, and a warm wind melted the snow-banks, so that the land was full of water. The young man and his Teacher made a birch-bark canoe, which floated upon the surface of the flood, while of the animals there were saved only a few, who had found a foothold upon the highest peaks.

The youth had now passed triumphantly through the various ordeals of his manhood. One day his Elder Brother spoke to him and said: "You have now conquered the animal people, and withstood the force of the elements. You have subdued the earth to your will, and still you are alone! It is time to go forth and find a woman whom you can love, and by whose help you may reproduce your kind."

"But how am I to do this?" replied the first man, who was only an inexperienced boy. "I am here alone, as you say, and I know not where to find a woman or a mate!"

"Go forth and seek her," replied the Great Teacher; and forthwith the youth set out on his wanderings in search of a wife. He had no idea how to make love, so that the first courtship was done by the pretty and coquettish maidens of the Bird, Beaver, and Bear tribes. There are some touching and whimsical love stories which the rich imagination of the Indian has woven into this old legend.

It is said, for example, that at his first camp he had built for himself a lodge of green boughs in the midst of the forest, and that there his reverie was interrupted by a voice from the wilderness—a voice that was irresistibly and profoundly sweet. In some mysterious way, the soul of the young man was touched as it had never been before, for this call of exquisite tenderness and allurement was the voice of the eternal woman!

Presently a charming little girl stood timidly at the door of his pine-bough wigwam. She was modestly dressed in gray, with a touch of jet about her pretty face, and she carried a basket of wild cherries which she shyly offered to the young man. So the rover was subdued, and love turned loose upon the world to upbuild and to destroy! When at last she left him, he peeped through the door after her, but saw only a robin, with head turned archly to one side, fluttering away among the trees.

His next camp was beside a clear, running stream, where a plump and industrious maid was busily at work chopping wood. He fell promptly in love with her also, and for some time they lived together in her cosy house by the waterside. After their boy was born, the wanderer wished very much to go back to his Elder Brother and to show him his wife and child. But the beaver-woman refused to go, so at last he went alone for a short visit. When he returned, there was only a trickle of water beside the broken dam, the beautiful home was left desolate, and wife and child were gone forever!

The deserted husband sat alone upon the bank, sleepless and faint with grief, until he was consoled by a comely young woman in glossy black, who took compassion upon his distress and soothed him with food and loving attentions. This was the bear-woman, from whom again he was afterward separated by some mishap. The story goes that he had children by each of his many wives, some of whom resembled their father, and these became the ancestors of the human race, while those who bore the characteristics of their mother returned to her clan. It is also said that such as were abnormal or monstrous in form were forbidden to reproduce their kind, and all love and mating between man and the animal creation was from that time forth strictly prohibited. There are some curious traditions of young men and maidens who transgressed this law unknowingly, being seduced and deceived by a magnificent buck deer, perhaps, or a graceful doe, and whose fall was punished with death.

The animal totems so general among the tribes were said to have descended to them from their great-grandmother's clan, and the legend was often quoted in support of our close friendship with the animal people. I have sometimes wondered why the scientific doctrine of man's descent has not in the same way apparently increased the white man's respect for these our humbler kin.

Of the many later heroes or Hiawathas who appear in this voluminous unwritten book of ours, each introduced an epoch in the long story of man and his environment. There is, for example, the Avenger of the Innocent, who sprang from a clot of blood; the ragged little boy who won fame and a wife by shooting the Red Eagle of fateful omen; and the Star Boy, who was the off-spring of a mortal maiden and a Star.

It was this last who fought for man against his strongest enemies, such as Wazeeyah, the Cold or North-Wind. There was a desperate battle between these two, in which first one had the advantage and then the other, until both were exhausted and declared a truce. While he rested, Star Boy continued to fan himself with his great fan of eagle feathers, and the snow melted so fast that North-Wind was forced to arrange a treaty of peace, by which he was only to control one half the year. So it was that the orderly march of the seasons was established, and every year Star Boy with his fan of eagle feathers sets in motion the warm winds that usher in the spring.

VI

ON THE BORDER-LAND OF SPIRITS

Death and Funeral Customs. The Sacred Lock of Hair. Reincarnation and the Converse of Spirits. Occult and Psychic Powers. The Gift of Prophecy.

The attitude of the Indian toward death, the test and background of life, is entirely consistent with his character and philosophy. Death has no terrors for him; he meets it with simplicity and perfect calm, seeking only an honorable end as his last gift to his family and descendants. Therefore he courts death in battle; on the other hand, he would regard it as disgraceful to be killed in a private quarrel. If one be dying at home, it is customary to carry his bed out of doors as the end approaches, that his spirit may pass under the open sky.

Next to this, the matter that concerns him most is the parting with his dear ones, especially if he have any little children who must be left behind to suffer want. His family affections are strong, and he grieves intensely for the lost, even though he has unbounded faith in a spiritual companionship.

The outward signs of mourning for the dead are far more spontaneous and convincing than is the correct and well-ordered black of civilization. Both men and women among us loosen their hair and cut it according to the degree of relationship or of devotion. Consistent with the idea of sacrificing all personal beauty and adornment, they trim off likewise from the dress its fringes and ornaments, perhaps cut it short, or cut the robe or blanket in two. The men blacken their faces, and widows or bereaved parents sometimes gash their arms and legs till they are covered with blood. Giving themselves up wholly to their grief, they are no longer concerned about any earthly possession, and often give away all that they have to the first comers, even to their beds and their home. Finally, the wailing for the dead is continued night and day to the point of utter voicelessness; a musical, weird, and heart-piercing sound, which has been compared to the, "keening" of the Celtic mourner.

The old-time burial of the Plains Indians was upon a scaffold of poles, or a platform among the boughs of a tree—their only means of placing the body out of reach of wild beasts, as they had no implements with which to dig a suitable grave. It was prepared by dressing in the finest clothes, together with some personal possessions and ornaments, wrapped in several robes, and finally in a secure covering of raw-hide. As a special mark of respect, the body of a young woman or a warrior was sometimes laid out in state in a new teepee, with the usual household articles and even with a dish of food left beside it, not that they supposed the spirit could use the implements or eat the food but merely as a last tribute. Then the whole people would break camp and depart to a distance, leaving the dead alone in an honorable solitude.

There was no prescribed ceremony of burial, though the body was carried out with more or less solemnity by selected young men, and sometimes noted warriors were the pall-bearers of a man of distinction. It was usual to choose a prominent hill with a commanding outlook for the last resting-place of our dead. If a man were slain in battle, it was an old custom to place his body against a tree or rock in a sitting position, always facing the enemy, to indicate his undaunted defiance and bravery, even in death.

I recall a touching custom among us, which was designed to keep the memory of the departed near and warm in the bereaved household. A lock of hair of the beloved dead was wrapped in pretty clothing, such as it was supposed that he or she would like to wear if living. This "spirit bundle," as it was called, was suspended from a tripod, and occupied a certain place in the lodge which was the place of honor. At every meal time, a dish of food was placed under it, and some person of the same sex and age as the one who was gone must afterward be invited in to partake of the food. At the end of a year from the time of death, the relatives made a public feast and gave away the clothing and other gifts, while the lock of hair was interred with appropriate ceremonies.

Certainly the Indian never doubted the immortal nature of the spirit or soul of man, but neither did he care to speculate upon its probable state or condition in a future life. The idea of a "happy hunting-ground" is modern and probably borrowed, or invented by the white man. The primitive Indian was content to believe that the spirit which the "Great Mystery" breathed into man returns to Him who gave it, and that after it is freed from the body, it is everywhere and pervades all nature, yet often lingers near the grave or "spirit bundle" for the consolation of friends, and is able to hear prayers. So much of reverence was due the disembodied spirit, that it was not customary with us even to name the dead aloud.

ON THE BORDER-LAND OF SPIRITS

It is well known that the American Indian had somehow developed occult power, and although in the latter days there have been many impostors, and, allowing for the vanity and weakness of human nature, it is fair to assume that there must have been some even in the old days, yet there are well-attested instances of remarkable prophecies and other mystic practice.

A Sioux prophet predicted the coming of the white man fully fifty years before the event, and even described accurately his garments and weapons. Before the steamboat was invented, another prophet of our race described the "Fire Boat" that would swim upon their mighty river, the Mississippi, and the date of this prophecy is attested by the term used, which is long since obsolete. No doubt, many predictions have been colored to suit the new age, and unquestionably false prophets, fakirs, and conjurers have become the pest of the tribes during the transition period. Nevertheless, even during this period there was here and there a man of the old type who was implicitly believed in to the last.

Notable among these was Ta-chank-pee Ho-tank-a, or His War Club Speaks Loud, who foretold a year in advance the details of a great war-party against the Ojibways. There were to be seven battles, all successful except the last, in which the Sioux were to be taken at a disadvantage and suffer crushing defeat. This was carried out to the letter. Our people surprised and slew many of the Ojibways in their villages, but in turn were followed and cunningly led into an ambush whence but few came out alive. This was only one of his remarkable prophecies.

Another famous "medicine-man" was born on the Rum River about one hundred and fifty years ago, and lived to be over a century old. He was born during a desperate battle with the Ojibways, at a moment when, as it seemed, the band of Sioux engaged were to be annihilated. Therefore the child's grandmother exclaimed: "Since we are all to perish, let him die a warrior's death in the field!" and she placed his cradle under fire, near the spot where his uncle and grandfathers were fighting, for he had no father. But when an old man discovered the new-born child, he commanded the women to take care of him, "for," said he, "we know not how precious the strength of even one warrior may some day become to his nation!"

This child lived to become great among us, as was intimated to the superstitious by the circumstances of his birth. At the age of about seventy-five years, he saved his band from utter destruction at the hands of their ancestral enemies, by suddenly giving warning received in a dream of the approach of a large war-party. The men immediately sent out scouts, and felled trees for a stockade, barely in time to meet and repel the predicted attack. Five years later, he repeated the service, and again saved his people from awful slaughter. There was no confusion of figures or omens, as with lesser medicine-men, but in every incident that is told of him his interpretation of the sign, whatever it was, proved singularly correct.

The father of Little Crow, the chief who led the "Minnesota massacre" of 1862, was another prophet of some note. One of his characteristic prophecies was made only a few years before he died, when he had declared that, although already an old man, he would go once more upon the war-path. At the final war-feast, he declared that three of the enemy would be slain, but he showed great distress and reluctance in foretelling that he would lose two of his own men. Three of the Ojibways were indeed slain as he had said, but in the battle the old war prophet lost both of his two sons.

There are many trustworthy men, and men of Christian faith, to vouch for these and similar events occurring as foretold. I cannot pretend to explain them, but I know that our people possessed remarkable powers of concentration and abstraction, and I sometimes fancy that such nearness to nature as I have described keeps the spirit sensitive to impressions not commonly felt, and in touch with the unseen powers. Some of us seemed to have a peculiar intuition for the locality of a grave, which they explained by saying that they had received a communication from the spirit of the departed. My own grandmother was one of these, and as far back as I can remember, when camping in a strange country, my brother and I would search for and find human bones at the spot she had indicated to us as an ancient burial-place or the spot where a lone warrior had fallen. Of course, the outward signs of burial had been long since obliterated.

The Scotch would certainly have declared that she had the "second sight," for she had other remarkable premonitions or intuitions within my own recollection. I have heard her speak of a peculiar sensation in the breast, by which, as she said, she was advised of anything of importance concerning her absent children. Other native women have claimed a similar monitor, but I never heard of one who could interpret it with such accuracy. We were once camping on Lake Manitoba when we received news that my uncle and his family had been murdered several weeks before, at a fort some two hundred miles distant. While all our clan were wailing and mourning their loss, my grandmother calmly bade them cease, saying that her son was approaching, and that they would see him shortly. Although we had no other reason to doubt the ill tidings, it is a fact that my uncle came into camp two days after his reported death.

At another time, when I was fourteen years old, we had just left Fort Ellis on the Assiniboine River, and my youngest uncle had selected a fine spot for our night camp. It was already after sundown, but my grandmother became unaccountably nervous, and positively refused to pitch her tent. So we reluctantly went on down the river, and camped after dark at a secluded place. The next day we learned that a family who were following close behind had stopped at the place first selected by my uncle, but were surprised in the night by a roving war-party, and massacred to a man. This incident made a great impression upon our people.

Many of the Indians believed that one may be born more than once, and there were some who claimed to have full knowledge of a former incarnation. There were also those who held converse with a "twin spirit," who had been born into another tribe or race. There was a well-known Sioux war-prophet who lived in the middle of the last century, so that he is still remembered by the old men of his band. After he had reached middle age, he declared that he had a spirit brother among the Ojibways, the ancestral enemies of the Sioux. He even named the band to which his brother belonged, and said that he also was a war-prophet among his people.

Upon one of their hunts along the border between the two tribes, the Sioux leader one evening called his warriors together, and solemnly declared to them that they were about to meet a like band of Ojibway hunters, led by his spirit twin. Since this was to be their first meeting since they were born as strangers, he earnestly begged the young men to resist the temptation to join battle with their tribal foes.

"You will know him at once," the prophet said to them, "for he will not only look like me in face and form, but he will display the same totem, and even sing my war songs!"

They sent out scouts, who soon returned with news of the approaching party. Then the leading men started with their peace-pipe for the Ojibway camp, and when they were near at hand they fired three distinct volleys, a signal of their desire for a peaceful meeting.

The response came in like manner, and they entered the camp, with the peace-pipe in the hands of the prophet.

Lo, the stranger prophet advanced to meet them, and the people were greatly struck with the resemblance between the two men, who met and embraced one another with unusual fervor.

It was quickly agreed by both parties that they should camp together for several days, and one evening the Sioux made a "warriors' feast" to which they invited many of the Ojibways. The prophet asked his twin brother to sing one of his sacred songs, and behold! it was the very song that he himself was wont to sing. This proved to the warriors beyond doubt or cavil the claims of their seer.

Such are the beliefs in which I was reared—the secret ideals which have nourished in the American Indian a unique character among the peoples of the earth. It simplicity, its reverence, its bravery and uprightness must be left to make their own appeal to the American of today, who is the inheritor of our homes, our names, and our tradition. Since there is nothing left us but remembered, at least let that remembrance be just!